Feely

and

Someone Else's Granny

Barbara Catchpole

Illustrated by Jan Dolby

Ransom

Hi I'm Feely and this is my diary.

There are six Feely books so far. It's best to read them in this order:

1   Feely's Magic Diary

2   Feely for Prime Minister

3   Feely and Her Well-Mad Parents

4   Feely Goes to Work

5   Feely and Henry VIII

6   Feely and Someone Else's Granny

Feely and Someone Else's Granny
by Barbara Catchpole
Illustrated by Jan Dolby

Published by Ransom Publishing Ltd.
Unit 7, Brocklands Farm, West Meon, Hampshire GU32 1JN, UK
www.ransom.co.uk

ISBN   978 1785911262
First published in 2016

❀❀ Monday

Dear Diary

This week I have learned a load of stuff

about old people. ❀❀

Now, I didn't like old people very much.

They are all baggy

They wear loads of

clothes all the time,

like a game of pass

the parcel – except

there's nothing nice

inside. ❀❀

Also they are very slow. You ask them

something and then you can write a whole

            ◦ ◦ ◦ ◦

5

homework essay before they answer. You think maybe they haven't heard you, or they've dozed off.

They push into queues just because they're old. Are they are afraid they might die before they reach the front?

Then they get to the front before you and spend ages fiddling in some stupid little purse to find exactly the right money.

Sometimes they drop a few coins on the floor, which they find very funny.

Especially when they can't bend down to pick them up.

They talk a lot to everyone as well (while they're ahead of you in the queue) and try to tell you all about their families. I don't care! I'm a stranger! I'm never going to see you ever again! (So you have a little

grand-daughter my age. So what? It's not
me, so don't talk to me!)

Also, and I'm trying to be fair, some of
them smell a bit of old person. I love the
smell of old books like
the ones you get in
charity shops for
20p, but I'm not
so keen on the
smell of old
person. Some
of them smell
a bit damp.

There's loads of stuff you can spray on
if you're a bit smelly. My brother, Ollie, who

is very smelly a lot of the time, sprays
stuff on over his shirt. My mum says he is
stuffing up the ozone layer all by himself.

So old people could do that. Spray a bit of
Lynx on, Grandad! And put some on the
inside of that huge mac, as well!

The other thing they do is run things into the back of your legs – shopping trolleys, those grubby tartan baskets on wheels and their great big mobility scooters.

Don't get me started on those scooters! There's an old people's home down the road and when they all go out in the morning on their scooters it's like a wrinklies' Grand

Prix. You have to stay off the pavement –
it's safer in the road!

OK, I'm banging on a bit.

So, of course, Mrs
Harding, our
Headteacher, had one
of her Great Ideas:
we should all talk to
our grandparents
about what happened in the 1950s, which
was before they had invented anything
good.

That woman does nothing but sit in her
lovely office having Great Ideas to make
our lives miserable. She never even comes

out to see the kids. Even the teachers have to key in a secret number and go down a really quiet corridor that's all offices to talk to her.

Has she ever *tried* to talk to an old person?

Now the 1950s do sound very

interesting. It was just after the war and

after the atomic bomb fell, and people were

getting their heads round the fact that

someone had used this massive weapon to

kill loads of people at the same time.

They thought the world would have to

change and they didn't know what would
happen. OLD mmmm

   But would we get any sense out of a
load of dopey old people if we asked them
about it? My teacher, Miss Rosy, really
seemed to think so!

   'Now, class, Mrs
Harding is very keen
on this, so I want you
all to try your very
hardest. Shane, if you
keep poking that rubber
up your nose, it will get stuck up there.
No, don't try to stuff it up someone else's
nose! What's the matter with you? I want

you all to ask your grandparents about this
very interesting time in history. Yes,
Hannah, I know you have more
grandparents than most people. Just
choose one! Which one do you like best?'

Hannah had loads of grandparents
because her grandad had been married
three times and her dad had been married

three times and her mum wasn't married to her dad any more. She has to carry a chart to keep track of it all.

I had a problem as well:

'I haven't got a grandparent I can talk to!'

'Oh, I'm sorry about that, Daphne!'

She still didn't know my name!

Miss Rosy thought my grandparents had gone to the Great Post Office Queue in the Sky. They hadn't.

One lot lived up in Scotland, where

there are loads of tiny insects you can't

see but you can feel them bite you.

They were Mum's parents and she

didn't ever phone them. She says if she

ever wants to have a headache, she'll bang

her head on the wall. It's cheaper.

The other pair was in Australia, and

they were never awake when we were.

'I'm sure you can find someone though!'

said Miss Rosy brightly, as if I could just go up to some random wrinkly in the Post Office and start talking about the atom bomb.

'OK, Miss,' I said. (There's no point arguing with her. She just does what she is told. If Mrs Harding told her to jump off the school roof, she'd go up there and do it.)

'And my name is Phoebe, or Feely, not Daphne.'

Saffron and her nasty little gang (I call them the Pink Click because they wear pink and Mum says they're a clique) — anyway, they called, 'Daphne, where's Scooby-Doo?' after me for the rest of the day.

Idiots!

TUESDAY

I told Mum about it all and she said she
would phone her mum and I could talk to
her.

I couldn't hear what
Gran said. This is
Mum's bit of the
conversation:

'Hello, Mum. Your daughter.
You only have one daughter.
Yes, Mark is fine. Yes, I'm still

married to him. Well, you were wrong,

weren't you? How are you?'

Then there was

a long bit where

Mum just said, 'Oh

dear' and, 'That's

doctors for you,'

and 'Nasty!' and

I got bored and

watched two

Spongebob Squarepants with the sound

down and the subtitles on.

'The thing is, Mum, Feely wants to talk

to you. Your granddaughter. Your only

granddaughter. She wants to ask you what

life was like in the nineteen fifties ... '

I heard the click as Grandma Bates

hung up.

click!

'She says she was busy in the 1950s

being a child and growing up into a

wonderful young woman so she could get

married and have an ungrateful daughter

who never phones her.'

horrible

Mum made that blowing air out noise that grown-ups make, like a balloon going down. 'Going to lie down. I've got a bit of a headache.'

You see! That's old people for you!

Wednesday

Today I decided to capture old Mrs Jones next door. She looks like she was alive in the 1950s. She's got a face like a road map, loads of lines that all meet up.

It took a bit of explaining, but then she

asked me to come in. We sat in the kitchen

and she gave me biscuits and milk.

Her house smells of soap and cats' pee,

and it's weird being in there because it's the

same as our house but completely different.

I was there for three hours and this

is what I learned:

1. The 1950s were very cold.

2. If you dunk your biscuit and a bit falls off, there's no way to get it out without a spoon. The milk tastes bitty, but it's OK.

3. Cats smell, even if you have a litter tray.

4. When cats use a litter tray, it's hard not to watch them.

5. In the 1950s televisions were just black and white. (The picture, that is. The tellies were

usually a kind of brown colour.)

6.   The bomb was a very bad thing.

(Really??)

And Mrs Jones blamed

scientists with mad hair (or it

might have been mad scientists

with hair,

because I was

so bored by

then I was

trying to

count the

poos in the litter tray. It's hard

'cos cats cover them up)

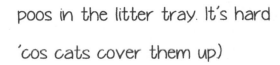

It was a little bit of progress, I suppose.

I had to look at old photos of Mrs Jones'

huge family (seventeen grandchildren – Dad

says they're like rabbits, but their teeth

looked OK to me) and I had to promise not

to squirt the hose at the cats any more.

Thursday

So on Monday I had to give my report in class and all I had was that televisions were black and white, it was cold, and the amazing news that a huge nuclear bomb was a bad thing.

Dad said just to Google it all and invent an old person. That seemed like loads of work because I'd have to write about how the old person felt, so it would be like writing a story at the same time.

Also I'd be lying, and I always go bright red and feel bad when I lie.

Me lying

No, what I needed was an oldie who had all their marbles and couldn't escape from me.

old

Then Mum had her Great Idea:

'Mrs Baggot! Of course! Mrs Baggot will do it! She's in the old peoples' home – she can't get away!'

That made the old people's home sound

great! Mrs Baggot is the grandmother of Tracy Baggot who sits at a desk in Mum's clinic and tells people where to go (she's not even any good at that).

Mum phoned Tracy and Tracy phoned the ~~prison~~ home. Then the nurse asked Mrs Baggot and Mrs Baggot said, OLD 'Alright, as long as she doesn't chew gum and I don't have to miss the bingo.'

And it was all set up for Saturday.

 **Friday**

Saffron said she got a great interview because her gran was a spy in the 1950s and spied on Adolf Hitler and she flew a fighter plane and she was in a submarine.

And I said,

'Didn't anyone tell her the war was

over by then?' and

'Am I bothered?' and

'My report is better than that!'

Then I felt really worried: my report

didn't exist.

Saturday

Today I went to the Sunnyside Home for Retired Gentlefolk. Only there was nothing 'gentle' about Mrs Baggot!

I had to sign a book in a sort of airlock. The door to the Old People Enclosure was locked.

I asked, 'Is that to stop people bothering Mrs Baggot?'

'You haven't met Mrs Baggot, have you?' said the nurse. 'That's to stop her bothering people.'

I looked for the sign that said 'Do Not Feed the Old People', but there wasn't one. Maybe an old person had eaten it.

The whole place smelled funny — like loo cleaner and hot air. Mrs Baggot's room was awesome though. There was random stuff everywhere — on the walls and on the tables — little pottery animals, things made out of shells, snow globes, photos in frames, kids' paintings, picture magnets all over the radiator.

It was just stuff everywhere.

Near the walls I could see last year's Christmas cards. There were piles of books on the floor and you had to work out how to get in there, like solving a puzzle.

Mrs Baggot was quite a large lady and she was wearing a huge purple dressing gown with a purple towel thing wrapped round her head.

She had two really big wooden walking sticks and she sat in the middle of the room like a giant purple spider.

When the nurse left me, I was quite
scared.

Mrs Baggot
hooked my arm
with the hook of
one of the sticks
and pulled me
towards her.

'Have you got the stuff? How are we
going to get out? How will we get past the
nurse? I've got to get out! I've got to get
out I tell you! I can't stand it any more!'

I was gobsmacked! She thought I could
get her out! What was I going to do?

I tried to say something, but I was just

opening and shutting my mouth. Mrs
Baggot started to cry — the purple dress
shook around her.

'Please don't cry ... ' I said, putting my
arm round her. Wait a
minute — she wasn't
crying, she was laughing —
great sobs of laughter. She
was laughing fit to bust!

She was winding me up!
And I fell for it! She was mean.

'Got you!' mmmmm old

It took quite a while for her to stop
laughing, and I had to find a tissue for her
to wipe her eyes.

'OK,' I said, trying to get back on track,

and remembering what Mum had said to do.

I had to be nice to the old bat – she was

my only hope.

'Thank you for seeing me, Mrs Baggot.

I am doing a project for my school. What

can you tell me about the 1950s, please?

Thank you.'

'Well, let me see,' she said, 'have you

brought me some chocolate? I'm not allowed it, you have to hide it. No chocolate! Useless brat! Anyway, let me see ... The 1950s. That was when we had loads of giant pink spiders and we all had to go up to Scotland to get away from them. Turns out they were from Mars ... '

She was really mean. And I was hot and fed up and Saffron was going to make fun of me. I could just see her and Stacey and Daff doing their silly girly giggles and pointing at me while I told the class that the 1950s were cold.  1950s

Why had I told Saffron that my report was better than hers? I couldn't do this! Before I knew what was happening, I was crying and shouting.

'You're a mean old lady! I need to get

this done! They will all make fun of me!
I hate you! I hate you!'

Mrs Baggot went very quiet. Then she
heaved herself to her feet. I didn't think
she was going to make it at one point, and
she looked like she might fall backwards, but
she made it.

'OK, brat,' she said, 'tell me all about it.'

So I did. I told her about how Saffron

and the Pink Click make fun of me. I told her about you, Diary, and how you are the only person I really talk to because Mum and Dad are always busy and Ollie is a boy.

I even told her about how Miss Rosy can't remember my name and Oliver pretended he had put my goldfish in the blender.

'What can I do about it all?' I asked, sniffing a bit.

'Nothing,' said Mrs Baggot,' Life sucks. Then you get old and it sucks some more.'

Then she told me all about the 1950s.

Nobody had a computer or a mobile phone. Old Mrs Jones was right — it was cold because loads of people had proper fire places in their houses and it got cold quickly if someone left the door to the room open.

TVs were just in black and white and they were tiny — and if they went wrong, you had to do without telly until you had enough money to get it fixed.

But sometimes if you banged the top of the telly with your fist it would fix itself.

Mrs Baggot's house had an outside toilet and she had to have a bath in a tin bath in front of the fire. Nobody could go into the room until you were finished!

You only had fresh stuff to eat because there weren't any freezers. She told me all about how people felt about the war and how people were still scared all the way through the 1950s because the war had been so horrible. (((((ooooom.

It was very interesting. I felt like I was really living through it. Mrs Baggot wrote loads of notes in my notebook for me in really neat writing that was all joined up.

Then Mrs Baggot said, 'I'm shattered – bog off now, brat!' and she fell asleep, just like that, in her chair, snoring like a pig.

I tip-toed out.

Monday!

Miss Rosy said my report was the best in the class. She said it was 'like totally real' – whatever that means!

Saffron kicked me on the leg as I went

up to get my Best in the Class Medal, but I didn't care.

pink

Everybody clapped me and I've got a certificate signed by Mrs Harding. I'm going to be a reporter when I grow up.

Tonight I am going to take Mrs Baggot a huge bar of chocolate hidden in an umbrella or something, like a spy, and show her my

medal.

Do you know what, Diary? I like her! She

is awesome!

About the author

Barbara Catchpole was a teacher for thirty years and enjoyed every minute. She has three sons of her own who were always perfectly behaved and never gave her a second of worry.

Barbara also tells lies.

How many have you read?

Magic Diary

Barbara Catchpole

for **Prime** **Minister**

Barbara Catchpole

and her **Well-Mad** Parents

Barbara Catchpole

How many have you read?

Feely Goes to Work

Feely and Henry VIII
Barbara Catchpole

Feely and Someone Else's Granny
Barbara Catchpole

Have you met
PIG?

Meet P.I.G – Peter Ian Green, although everybody calls him PIG for short. PIG lives with his mum.

He is small for his age, but says his mum is huge for hers. She is a single mum, but PIG says she looks more like a double mum or even a treble mum.

PIG and the Ice-cream Cake
Barbara Catchpole

PIG Skives off School
Barbara Catchpole

PIG is a Blue Baboon's Bottom
Barbara Catchpole

PIG SuperPig!
Barbara Catchpole

PIG and the Baldy Cat
Barbara Catchpole

PIG Leaves Home (for a bit)
Barbara Catchpole

PIG Whopping Great Fib

PIG is Harry Snotter
Barbara Catchpole

PIG and the Rainbow Hair
Barbara Catchpole

PIG and the Big Quiz
Barbara Catchpole

PIG Gets Angry
Barbara Catchpole

PIG's Season's Finale
Barbara Catchpole